The Hard Fall

The Hard Fall

Brenda Chapman

Anna Sweet Mysteries

GRASS ROOTS PRESS

First published in 2013 by Grass Roots Press

Grass Roots Press gratefully acknowledges the financial support for its publishing programs provided by the following agencies: the Government of Canada through the Canada Book Fund and the Government of Alberta through the Alberta Foundation for the Arts.

Library and Archives Canada Cataloguing in Publication

Chapman, Brenda, 1955–, author
    The hard fall / Brenda Chapman.

(Anna Sweet mysteries)
ISBN 978–1–77153–005–7 (pbk.)

    I. Title. II. Series: Chapman, Brenda, 1955– Anna Sweet mysteries.

PS8605.H36H37 2013   C813'.6   C2013–904395–0

Printed and bound in Canada.

For my daughters, Lisa and Julia

I lowered the camera and checked the clock on my car's dashboard. Six p.m. on the dot. I was about to wrap up my first case as a PI and feeling mighty pleased with myself. A cold beer and a plate of nachos would help me to celebrate. I reached for my cellphone.

Jada Price, my new partner in solving crime at Storm Investigations, picked up on the first ring. "So, what you got, Agent 007?" she asked.

"Just solved that insurance fraud case. I'm ready to kick up my heels."

"I told you that you were a natural at getting the dirt on people." Jada's voice lost its lightness. "I need you to come to the office, though. A new case has come in. I'm working on that divorce stakeout so it's up to you. But I'm not sure you'll want to take this one."

"Oh?" I asked. "I thought you said our bank account says we can't be choosy."

"This job will be thankless. Storm Investigations might look stupid just for taking it on. I'll fill you in as soon as you get here."

"On my way," I said. I tossed my phone onto the passenger seat and started my Chevy Sonic. I'd leased it for a year as a business expense. Unless more work rolled in, I would soon be returning it to the dealer and getting back on the city bus. The new case had to be a real loser if Jada was thinking about turning it down.

I drove slowly up Richmond Road past restaurants, clothing stores, and coffee and tea shops. Night was settling in already. It was the first week of October and chilly in the evenings. I thought about stopping in at Whispers Pub for that plate of nachos and a beer. But I kept going—past a string of condos, across Parkdale Avenue, and into our neighbourhood, Hintonburg. Jada wouldn't be too pleased if I kept her waiting.

For once, I found a parking spot in the same block as our office on Wellington Street. Most stores were closed for the night, and it was early for the dinner crowd. We'd rented two tiny rooms on the second floor of a commercial building. A thrift shop and a takeout pizza place were down below. Gino Roma waved at me as I walked by on my way to the stairs. He was tossing pizza dough in front of the wood-burning oven. He kept trying to set me up with his son Nick. So far, I'd resisted.

When I entered our office, Jada was sitting at the desk facing the door. A young woman in a navy blue suit sat across from her. Both faces turned to look at me. The woman stood and held out her hand.

"I'm Rosie Brown," she said. "You must be Anna Sweet."

I looked past her shoulder to Jada. I was trying to get a read on whether Rosie Brown was the case we didn't want to take. Jada kept her face blank. "Pleased to meet you," I said finally, shaking Rosie's hand.

"Pull up a chair," Jada said. "Ms. Brown is here because she needs someone to do some digging for her firm's client."

I grabbed a chair from the other office and sat between the two of them. Rosie was young. Maybe twenty-five. Her eyes were sparkly blue behind large black-framed glasses. She'd pulled her blond hair back into a bun, probably trying to look older.

She leaned toward me. "I'm with Jones, Jones, and Lockhart. I'm assisting Greg Jones Junior in defending a murder suspect. Sadly, the file is not going as planned."

Jada cleared her throat. "You might have heard of the case, Anna," she said in a deadpan voice. "The Crown versus Paul Taylor."

My eyes opened wide, as if I'd been poked with a cattle prod. Jada was right. This was not a case we wanted to get involved in. I said, "Front page news every day since August. Six weeks since the murder and people still can't get enough of the story. Odds-makers say he's going to get life. Open and shut. No other suspects."

Rosie Brown frowned. "Yeah, I know what the press is saying. Our client is innocent, however. We hired another PI but he didn't come up with anything helpful."

"Maybe because there was nothing to find," Jada said mildly. Her black eyes met mine.

"We don't think the investigator tried hard enough," Rosie said. Her eyes flashed. "My client has agreed to pay a higher fee. His money won't be worth anything to him if he gets life."

"Not many places to spend a fortune in Sing Sing," I agreed. "So what kind of money are we talking?" I could have pussy footed around and waited for her to state an amount. But it was late and I was tired.

"Seven hundred a day and a bonus fifty thousand if you find something to get him off."

Jada whistled. "We'll take it . . . I mean, Anna will take on the case. We can't promise results, though."

I shot Jada a "thanks a lot" stare, but I didn't say anything. We had to make money or we'd lose our office. And we had to have an office to run a PI business. The law was clear on that.

Rosie's face relaxed into a smile. "Great. I have a contract ready. I also copied a list of facts and witnesses for you." She whipped a stack of paper out of her briefcase before we could change our minds. She set it on the desk and handed me a pen. "Paul is being held in the detention centre without bail. He's expecting you early tomorrow morning. We have a week before the trial begins. We'll need something before then to prove his innocence."

"No problem," I said. "I'm sure . . ."

Jada met my eyes. The shake of her head made me close my mouth before I said the rest. It didn't stop me from thinking it, though.

. . . *there are some flying pigs out there somewhere.*

CHAPTER TWO

I drove through side streets until I reached the Parkway, which ran next to the canal. If it had still been light, I would have been treated to fall colours in all their glory: red, yellow, and orange leaves against a deep blue sky. Now, I saw only dark tree trunks and street lights shining off the river of black water. I found this route to Dad's house in Alta Vista soothing after a tiring day. The long, winding drive gave me time to think.

Like the rest of Ottawa, I had followed the Paul Taylor murder case on the nightly news. Katie and Paul were the closest thing Ottawa had to the rich and famous. Paul was a well-off business man and city councillor. He was married to Katie Taylor, a once-famous model from New York City. They lived in a big house in Rockcliffe and travelled in all the best circles. A charmed life, that is until six months ago when their maid found neighbour Laura Flint dead in their king-sized bed.

Turns out Laura and Paul Taylor had been having an affair. The papers suggested that he tried to end it that fateful August morning, and Laura threatened to tell Katie. From all accounts, Paul went into a rage and killed poor Laura Flint by smothering her with a pillow. He'd then put on clean clothes and joined his friends for a round of golf.

The papers reported that Katie was visiting her mother in Toronto at the time of the murder. Paul was arrested and put in jail awaiting trial. The police could find no other suspects. His high-powered friends slipped away. The mayor put him on temporary leave until his name was cleared. Nobody expected him to be back. The Taylor name was quietly removed from his business. The only one to stand by him was his wife Katie. The reporters urged her to drop her cold-blooded, killer husband. She refused. Everyone figured that Katie would dump him when she came to her senses. The public agreed that until then, she deserved our pity.

And now, I was going to try to find evidence to set free the most hated man in the city.

••••••••••

I pulled into Dad's driveway twenty minutes later. I sat for a moment in the dark. I could see Dad's bowed head in the lamplight through the front window. He had on his reading glasses and was sitting in his favourite leather chair. I imagined he was reading a history book about one war or another. He'd spent thirty-five years in the armed forces and loved reading about past conflicts. I was just happy to see him out of bed.

I jumped out of my car and hurried into the house.

"There you are," he said when I entered the living room. He lowered the book onto his lap. "I was beginning to think you were out on a hot date."

"No such luck. Did Cheri come by?" My sister and I had been taking turns keeping Dad company after each round of chemo. He said he didn't want us to bother. We ignored his commands to leave him alone. I think he was secretly pleased that we fussed.

"She was here but I sent her home after lunch. I should be good now for another week until the next round."

"A week to fatten you up. I'll scramble some eggs and serve them up on toast if you're hungry."

"Only if you join me."

"Of course. I can't let you get fat alone."

Dad gave me a quick smile. He knew that I was covering my concern with lame humour.

I told Dad about my new case while we ate at the kitchen table. Dad had followed the story in the paper like everyone else in Ottawa. Everyone, that is, except me. I'd heard bits and pieces, of course. But starting a business and looking after Dad and his house had kept me busy the last few months. I hadn't had time to wade into the Taylors' backgrounds or to read up on the juicy gossip.

"The Taylors don't have any kids," Dad said. "He's the CEO of a company that made millions building helicopters. His big plant is outside Kingston but the head office is here. He was elected to city council last year. She used to be a swimsuit model but gave that up to marry him. Two of the beautiful people. It's like watching a train wreck."

"What about his mistress, Laura Flint? Do you know anything about her?"

"Her husband died in a hunting accident some years back. Not sure where they lived, but I seem to remember it was out west. She moved into one of those fancy houses in Rockcliffe, so she's not hurting for money. I guess that's how she met the Taylors."

"Beware of rich widows," I said. I stood and took our empty plates to the counter. "Can I get you anything else, Dad?"

Dad stretched his arms over his head. He'd lost weight and it hurt to look at him too closely. "Think I'll call it a night. How about I do some fact-finding for you tomorrow on my computer? Might be of some use putting together your case, given all my work experience."

"That would be a big help. I have some files from Taylor's lawyer to go through tonight. I'll leave a list of names for you to run searches on." Dad had worked in military intelligence the last part of his career. He'd spent a lot of time searching for information on computers.

"Consider it done."

From the kitchen, I watched Dad walk with ramrod-straight back. No matter how much pain he was in, he never let on. The Sweets never let on. I leaned on the counter and closed my eyes for a moment. When I heard him climb into his bed, I opened my eyes and blinked away the blurriness. I gave myself a shake. Dad was going to make it through. I just had to keep the faith. He would accept no less from the daughter he raised in his likeness.

Never show your underbelly. If you're hurting, suck it up.

The Sweet family motto. The words we live by, until death do us part.

CHAPTER THREE

Paul Taylor sat across the table from me in the meeting room. He wore an orange jump suit and handcuffs. He held himself like a man used to being in charge, but I saw signs of wear. His silver hair had grown just shaggy enough to let me know he wasn't getting two-hundred-dollar haircuts in jail. His eyes were piercing blue but tired. They studied me. He had a poker face; I couldn't tell what he was thinking.

"I'm sorry to have to make you repeat everything," I said. "I'm going to examine every bit of evidence again. I'd like to start with you and Laura Flint."

"A bad decision on my part," Paul said.

"Excuse me?"

"To start up with her. I didn't kill her."

"I'm keeping an open mind. Tell me how the two of you met." He nodded when I showed him my tape recorder. I pressed play and set it on the table between us.

"Laura moved in next door about six months ago. We used to meet walking the dogs. Chatted about the weather, dog grooming, nothing stuff. Then she started talking about her husband and how hard his death hit her. She'd tried to forget by travelling to far off places. It helped a bit, but she was lonely. We started planning our walks and going for coffee. I swear I never thought of her as anything but a friend. Katie was restless at home so she went back to work last fall. Most of her jobs were out of town. In fact, she was gone most of May and June on location. I know that doesn't excuse me sleeping with Laura. I just fell into it. It was a stressful time and Laura was there to listen. I was alone . . . a lot."

"Did Katie know?"

He answered quickly. Maybe too quickly. "No. She quit taking work in July and talked about starting a family. I'm older than her. It had been one of our sticking points. I wanted children but she didn't. I thought that we were going in the same direction at last. I told Laura we had to stop seeing each other. She accepted it, no big deal. At least I thought so."

"You and Katie had problems before she started working out of town?"

"Some. Yeah. We'd grown apart the year before. I still loved her and didn't want to lose her. Needless to say, I was thrilled when she wanted to start a family. It felt like a new beginning. We planned a summer-long holiday in Spain to make a baby. Laura's murder put an end to that."

"How did Katie react when she found out you'd been sleeping with Laura? I know it came out after the murder."

"Katie was hurt, but she understood. She said she'd stand by me because she knows I'm not a killer. I might have made mistakes, but I love my wife more than breathing. Katie knows that."

"The maid found Laura dead in your bed. Do you have any idea how she got there?"

He shook his head. "It was Saturday. A beautiful August day and I had an early tee-off time. The police arrested me at the club house at noon. Katie was visiting her family in Toronto. I have no idea what Laura was doing in my bed—or how she got into the house."

"I heard that your company wants to buy you out."

The flash of anger in his eyes was the first sign of real emotion that I'd seen. He quickly covered it by looking down at his hands. "Gordon and Kyle.

Yeah, I've heard. But I'll let those backstabbers buy the company if I'm found guilty. I want Katie to be taken care of."

"I wonder why you'd have two guys like them working for you." I threw out the statement, hoping to see more of his anger. Until now, he'd been doing what got him elected: hiding what he felt behind an unreadable face.

"I've known Gordon since we were in university together. He's bright but not good at getting his ideas off the ground." Paul shrugged. His blue eyes stared into mine. "Lately, he'd started resenting me. We were arguing about money."

"How so?"

"He wanted a bigger cut of the profits. Bottom line is that he'd be nowhere without me. I didn't owe Gordon anything more than what he got."

"What about Kyle?"

"Kyle has less business sense than Gordon. He's not as concerned about making money as Gordon. He's more of a follower. Gordon is the brains in that duo."

The guard knocked on the window. My time was up. I turned off the tape recorder and stood to leave. "I'll start looking into your case," I said. "Try not to give up."

"I haven't, but it's not easy." He sent me the first smile since I arrived. A quick smile with no joy behind it. It hinted at the charm that must have won over both Katie and Laura.

I walked across the parking lot to my car. A breeze had come up and leaves swirled around my feet. Clouds were moving in. It would be raining before night fall. Paul Taylor was probably in his cell with a long day ahead. He might or might not have any faith in me getting him out.

That was okay with me. I didn't have much faith either. But it wouldn't stop me from trying.

CHAPTER FOUR

I stopped at a Tim Hortons to get coffee and a bran muffin. I also wanted to check in with Dad. He was working on his laptop in bed when I reached him on the phone.

"How are you today?" I asked.

"Just fine. I've been looking up stories on Laura Flint. She was not on the hunting trip when her husband got shot. Doesn't say who pulled the trigger. I intend to track the shooter down." He sounded full of energy for the first time in a long time.

"Good." I didn't think the information would help with my case but it would keep Dad busy. "I'm on my way to check out the Taylor home and talk with Katie. She's waiting for me to arrive."

"I'll let you know if I find anything of use." Dad abruptly ended the call.

I tucked my phone into my pocket. I looked out the window at the rain sliding down the glass.

Heavy clouds overhead made the day feel dark and depressing. I was chilled from my walk from the jail to my car. I promised myself a hot soak in the tub when I got home, whenever that was.

··········

Rockcliffe was a rich neighbourhood east of downtown and south of the Ottawa River. It was filled with old shady trees and flowering shrubs and had the feel of an overgrown garden. There were no sidewalks; the narrow streets just wound past ten-million-dollar houses and sprawling estates.

The Taylors and Laura Flint lived next door to each other on Park Street. A row of cedar hedges separated their properties. Laura had lived in a modest—by Rockcliffe standards—two-storey house, red brick with blue shutters. The Taylors owned the larger of the two homes: grey brick, black shutters, slate roof, and three-car garage. I pulled into their circular driveway and parked. Dad's house could fit into the garage, no problem. I had a feeling that Katie Taylor and I were not going to be soul sisters.

The maid led me into a back sunroom where Katie stood framed in the window. She was taller than my five foot nine and much more slender. She looked elegant in a silk blouse, tight black skirt, and red high heels. Her black hair fell in waves to her shoulders. Her eyes, when she turned to look at me, were an unusual jade green.

Katie glided across the floor and took my hand in both of hers. "Thank you so much for taking on Paul's case," she said. Even her voice was beautiful: low and husky. Paul Taylor must have been *very* lonely to cheat on this goddess.

We sat facing each other in matching blue chairs. "Can I get you some tea?" she asked.

"No, thank you. I just have a few questions."

"Of course. Ask anything. I want to say before you start, I believe that Paul is innocent. He made a mistake sleeping with Laura. That doesn't make him a killer." Her eyes shimmered with unshed tears.

"He's lucky to have your support." I opened my notebook. "The maid says that the doors were locked when she arrived that morning. How could Laura have gotten in if Paul hadn't opened the door?"

"I . . . I'm not sure." Katie's voice got stronger. "She must have though. Paul told me that he didn't let her in. I believe him."

"I understand you were in Toronto at the time of the murder."

"I'd gone to visit my mother. She's in a nursing home. Dementia."

"So you would have signed in and out?"

"No. It's not a prison. It's a small, expensive group home. And my mother still looks after herself for the most part." Katie's bottom lip trembled. "I know she won't be able to for much longer."

"Okay." I made a note to check into her visit. "What was Laura Flint like?"

"Oh, quiet. Sort of a mouse." Katie leaned forward. "Not Paul's type at all."

I'd seen photos of a smiling Laura Flint in the paper. I'd also seen the photos of her dead. She'd been attractive enough—petite with a big chest, blue eyes, and long, straight brown hair. I inhaled Katie's perfume. It reminded me of summer roses and ice wine. Sweet and expensive. "You weren't angry about the affair?"

She flicked her hand in front of her face. "Of course I was, but not for long. Paul begged me to forgive him and I did. He is a good man and she took advantage. We still love each other."

"Had you known they were sleeping together before she was killed?"

"No."

I held my lips together tightly. I had loved someone who also cheated. And Jimmy was now married to my sister, Cheri. Not only was Katie beautiful, if she truly forgave Paul she was also a saint. There's no way I could have done that.

"One last question," I said. "Do you have any idea of who could have killed Laura?"

Katie didn't answer right away. When she did, her voice was sad. "No. I can't think of anybody." She stared at me with her big green eyes. They were full of secrets and shadows. They seemed to be telling me that her husband *had* killed Laura Flint. Or at least that there was something more to the story. She just wasn't going to admit it out loud.

"I'd like to see the bedroom where Laura was killed."

"The police already . . ."

"I know, but it would help me to see the crime scene."

"Upstairs. The door is closed at the end of the hall. I haven't been able to bring myself to go in since they took the body away."

CHAPTER FIVE

I found nothing of interest in the bedroom or Paul's home office. I hadn't expected to. The Ottawa Police had made a clean sweep of evidence, including papers and computers. Rosie Brown had shared copies of the reports that included photos of the crime scene.

Katie walked me to the front door when I was done my search. She stood on the landing and waited while I walked down the steps. When I turned to look up at her, she gave a brave smile and a wave. I was again struck by her effortless beauty. Even with her husband facing murder charges, she looked stunning enough to pose for a magazine cover.

I stepped around puddles on my way to look at Laura Flint's property. I followed her driveway lined in bushes and trees toward the front door. The rain had slowed to a drizzle—just enough to make me damp and chilled. Somebody had cut Laura's grass in the front yard and raked up the leaves from two oak trees. I spotted a house for sale sign near the road. Of course. She'd lived alone and it would be sold as part of the estate. I made a note of the real estate agent. Whoever was behind the sale might have information about Laura. Hopefully, they were a family member.

I rang the front doorbell. I jumped up and down trying to get warm while I waited. Nobody came and I tried knocking. Nothing. I thought about picking the lock but didn't want to chance it ... yet. I'd try the legal route first.

· · · · · · · · · ·

The hamburger and fries from my late lunch sat heavy in my stomach when Detective Johnny Shaw walked into his office at the Ottawa Police Headquarters. I'd phoned ahead and he'd agreed to see me, but not because he wanted to. The Taylor case was a hot potato, and he really had no choice.

Shaw dropped into his desk chair and looked me up and down like a murder suspect. I was leaning against the filing cabinet, pretending not to notice. I was trying not to think of how much I disliked him.

"Didn't figure I'd be seeing you back here," he said. "How's it going, Sweet?"

"Oh, you know. It's going."

This was about as good as it got between Shaw and me. He'd led the grilling I faced after I shot and killed a fourteen-year-old kid high on drugs. It was the event that made me end my short career on the force. I was cleared but would never forget how much Shaw enjoyed making me squirm. He was built like a bear with hulking shoulders and hands the size of baseball gloves. He rarely smiled. His nickname was "Ice Cube" because he was about as cold as one.

"You looked into the Laura Flint murder," I said.

"Yeah. Married boyfriend did it."

"His lawyer has hired me to give the case another look."

"Good luck with that. Paul Taylor's going to get life. He might be a smart business man and big deal city councillor, but he's stupid as killers go. Crimes of passion never work in the killer's favour. Too messy." Shaw scowled. "Taking this case isn't going to make you look too smart either, Sweet."

I decided to ignore the jab, since the same thought had crossed my mind more than once. "Have you got a file on Laura Flint that you can share?"

"What, now you're going to make it look like she deserved what she got?"

"No. I want to speak with her family and friends. She might have had other enemies."

Shaw's top lip lifted. For him, this was as good as a belly laugh. "Yeah, right. Somebody else got her naked in Taylor's bed and held a pillow over her face. She lay there and took it. Keep chasing down *that* lead. You're going to look like a genius."

"Doesn't it seem strange to you that if Taylor killed her, he just left her in his bed? Don't you think he'd at least try to cover up his crime?"

Something shifted in Shaw's eyes. I could tell that I'd hit on a loose end that still bothered him. We both knew Taylor wasn't a stupid man. Leaving Laura in his bed in his locked house didn't make sense.

Shaw let out his breath, long and slow. "Who knows why people act like they do after a murder? All I know is that Taylor's the only one with both motive and opportunity." He typed on his keyboard for a minute. Then he stood and looked down at me. "I'm going on break for half an hour. If you want to stick around and wait, that's up to you." He swung his screen around so that I could read Laura Flint's file.

"Thanks, Shaw," I said. "I owe you one."

"No, now I figure we're even." His pale blue eyes met mine. I almost thought I saw regret in their depths. I didn't know whether it was for the grilling five years ago or the thankless job I was doing now. Either way, I would take what he was offering. I had nothing else.

CHAPTER SIX

Jada was sound asleep on the couch in our office. A newspaper covered her face. Her hands were crossed on her chest as if she'd been praying. I nudged her arm. The paper fell to the floor when she sat up. She gave me a sleepy grin.

"What a case I'm on. I spent the night chasing after Dick—he would be the husband—and his buddies. They must have hit every strip club between here and hell."

"Did Dick the husband do anything that would make his wife leave him?"

"Two lap dances but nothing else. Not enough to end his marriage. I'm going to have to keep following."

"Maybe this will be one of those cases that renews your faith in husbands and wives."

Jada shook her short black locks and held out her hand. I took it and pulled her to standing position. "Next you're going to tell me you still believe in the tooth fairy. Your trust in people is refreshing, Anna Sweet. Misplaced, but refreshing."

She crossed to our little fridge and took out two beers. We put the desk chairs side by side and popped the caps. Before taking a swallow, we both leaned back and put our feet on the desk.

"So, any progress on the Taylor file?" she asked.

"Not really. I've got the name of Laura Flint's cousin to follow up on tomorrow. Means a drive to Perth in the morning. Taylor also has two vice presidents in his company who turned on him pretty quickly. If nothing pans out with them, I'm afraid Paul Taylor looks guilty as sin. Even his lovely wife believes he did it, from what I read in her eyes."

"You're focusing on the victim?"

"I'm going to look at her life as well as Taylor's. If he didn't kill her, then somebody in her life had a reason."

"Well, drag it out. Every day makes us that much richer." Jada took a long drink from her bottle. "What do you think about hiring an office manager?"

I looked around. We had a used desk, three chairs, a couch, and a beer fridge. The other room was still empty. We weren't exactly on easy street. "Do you think we need one?"

"We could try someone out to drum up business."

"So we would need someone with people, marketing, and accounting skills who works well alone. Also, they should have another income because this one won't be enough to cover their rent."

"I'm just saying, if we want to make money, we've got to spend some. The right person could get us cases by promoting our services. They could run this office while you and I are working cases."

I thought it over. Jada had been an Ottawa cop, too. She'd gotten tired of being the token black female handing out parking tickets. This business meant more to her than it did to me. I was hanging around for the year until my father was feeling better. At least, that's what I told myself. I knew I should care more than I did about making our business grow. It might also make it easier for me to leave if Jada wasn't alone.

"Okay," I said. "Let's get someone." I drank the last of my beer and patted her knee. "Time to go home and make my dad's supper."

Jada's wide smile was enough to make me feel guilty. "I'm going to catch a bit more sleep before I'm back on Dick the husband watch. I sure hope he stays home tonight. The guy loves to party."

"You're getting old, Jada Price. Was a time you liked to party, too."

"I still like a good time. Just not in strip clubs, biker bars, and pool halls."

"Where is his wife when he's out playing with his buddies?"

"Working night shift in a seniors home. He works nine to five selling cars and has his evenings free."

"Great way to keep the love alive."

"Isn't it just? This job is going to make me swear off men."

I put my feet on the floor and stood up. "I'm way ahead of you there. I swore off them years ago."

....

I'd parked my car on a side street some distance from our office. I set out with my head down, thinking about the pictures of Laura Flint's body. She'd looked as if she was sleeping, not dead. Like she would wake up at any moment. Her photos brought home the tragedy more than anything else.

I reached the corner and heard footsteps running behind me. I stopped to wait for a couple of cars to pass. I turned my head to glance over my shoulder at the person jogging by. I briefly saw a man in black sweatpants and a black hoodie bearing down on me. I had no time to react; no time to be afraid. His hand shoved hard into my back on his way past. I stumbled off the curb. My arms reached out wildly as I fell onto my knees on the road. The driver of a white Mazda leaned on his horn. The car swerved into the oncoming lane, tires squealing, just missing me by inches. The driver sped off without waiting to see if I was okay.

I rolled back toward the curb, trying to flatten myself against it. I heard the next car getting closer. It came very near but screeched to a stop. I heard doors slamming and then saw the driver and his passenger race over. Two pairs of hands lifted me onto the sidewalk. They helped me to stand. My knees and hands throbbed from the impact of striking the pavement. I put weight on my legs. Nothing was broken.

"You could have been killed," the woman said. She didn't release her hold around my waist. She sounded terrified.

"Should we call an ambulance?" the man asked. He was white haired and had shocked grey eyes.

"No. No. I'm fine," I said. I looked down the street. The jogger was gone. "Did you see the man who pushed me?" I asked.

"Somebody pushed you?" the woman said. She looked in the same direction that I was looking. Then, she turned to the man. "I didn't see him. Did you, George?"

He shook his head. "You should report this to the police."

"What is this world coming to?" the woman asked. "We're not safe in the middle of the day in our own city."

"I'm okay," I said. "He must not have seen me. I'm sure it was an accident."

"Well, he could have stopped after you fell. He couldn't have missed the horn honking and the car tires squealing."

The couple left me after they were certain I was all right. I limped back to my car where I checked the scrapes on my hands and knees. I was going to have bruises. I sat for a while in the driver's seat until the pain lessened. The attack had left me shaken, but also angry. It had felt personal. Was somebody trying to keep me from digging into the Flint murder? Had I scared somebody enough to want me dead?

. . . .

Cheri's new black BMW was sitting in Dad's driveway when I arrived home at seven. I found a place to park on the street four houses down. It would have been nice to keep driving around until my sister left, but Dad might need saving. My knees also needed some attention.

Evan opened the front door as I climbed the steps. "Aunt Anna! You were so late that Mom made spaghetti for supper. I set the table."

I ruffled his blond hair and bent down for a hug. I whispered in his ear, "Did she remember to boil the water before putting in the pasta?"

"I made sure this time," he whispered back.

"How many days before you turn six?"

"Three days until my party!"

"If you're this smart at five, look out six. Your dad on evening shift?"

"Yup."

I breathed a sigh of relief. It had been nearly six years since Jimmy and I were a couple. I'd been gone from Ottawa for five of those years. I still felt awkward whenever I saw him. It was hard to see my sister married to the man I'd planned to spend my life with.

Evan and I walked into the kitchen. Dad was sitting at the table typing on his laptop. I went to the freezer and got a couple of ice packs.

"What happened to you?" Dad asked.

"Just had a tumble on the sidewalk," I said. I sat down at the table next to Dad and held the packs on my knees. They felt cool on my sore hands.

Cheri began scooping tomato sauce onto plates of spaghetti. "A little sticky," she said, "but we won't be hungry later. Here, Evan. Serve your grandpa." She handed him a plate.

Cheri brought over the other three plates of spaghetti, and she and Evan took their places at the table. Dad was the first to brave a forkful of pasta. His eyes got wider as he started chewing.

"What did you add to the canned sauce, Cheri?" he gasped with his mouth full.

"A few spices from your cupboard and some leftovers from the fridge. Do you like it?"

"Um hum." He kept chewing the same mouthful while he tried to drink from his water glass.

I stood. "Why don't I open that red wine we were saving, Dad? We also have some buns and peanut butter around here somewhere."

Dad and Evan nodded. Cheri glared at me. Then she tasted the sauce and pushed away her plate. She reached for Dad's plate. "Okay, this is disgusting. I'll order pizza."

Evan giggled.

....

Evan started yawning at nine o'clock. Cheri told him it was time to head home and she hugged us goodbye. I returned to the kitchen after walking them to the front door.

"I thought they'd never leave," Dad said. He was already back to hitting keys on his laptop.

I set a cup of tea next to him on the kitchen table and sat down. I'd left the tea steeping while I saw Cheri and Evan out. "Find anything interesting?"

"It seems the person who shot Roger Flint while hunting in the bush outside Calgary was never found. The police tested the guns of the two people hunting with him. Both came up clean."

"Wow. If it was an accident, why didn't somebody come forward?"

"My thought exactly. That's why I phoned an army buddy who is now retired in Calgary. He had an interest in the case because Laura Flint and his daughter went to school together."

"Did he give you any information about Laura and her family?"

Dad smiled. "Laura was adopted by the Hills when she was three years old. She was a wild teenager and married Roger Flint when she was seventeen, right out of high school. Roger was older and owned a home and a restaurant. She'd been one of his part-time waitresses."

"Marrying the owner is one way to get out of waiting tables," I said.

"Three years later, he wound up dead. Laura sold up and left town. Word was she moved around a lot, living the high life."

"Did she have a new man in her life?"

"No way of knowing, although rumour was that she did. She was cleared of shooting Roger, by the way. She was nowhere near the woods."

"I wonder how she landed in Ottawa." It seemed like an odd choice for a woman who'd had her pick of cities.

"Her cousin Maddie Ringer and Maddie's husband Allan live in Perth, an hour from the city."

"And I'll be paying them a visit tomorrow," I said. "A cop friend gave me the address. Sorry, Dad, but I have to go to bed. It's been a long day."

"I'll just finish up a few more leads. Go ahead and get some shut eye."

I stopped at the door leading into the hallway. Dad's face was lit up by the computer screen. His eyes had regained their sharp blue intensity. His lips moved as he silently read whatever he'd pulled up on the screen. He reached over to jot down something on a notepad he kept nearby.

Sometimes, like right now, I allowed myself to believe that everything was going to work out okay. Dad was going to recover and get back to his old, crusty self. I'd finish out my year with Jada as promised. Then I'd leave this city and everyone in it far behind. I'd continue my life on the road right where I left off.

CHAPTER SEVEN

The little town of Perth was an hour's drive if traffic was moving well. I set out after making Dad's breakfast. The rain from the day before had moved on but the air was still cool. Winter would be blowing into town soon. I'd spent the last five winters in the southern States, and my wardrobe ran to bathing suits, sandals, and shorts. The first snowfall was going to be a shock to my system.

I was twenty minutes outside of Perth when I spotted a black car with a tinted windshield behind me. At first, I thought nothing of it. Then I noticed that the driver was keeping a few car lengths back. The white van behind me turned off, and the black car fell further back. The driver let another car pass. *Odd*.

I sped up and passed two cars. I checked my rear view mirror. The black car had passed the car that had just passed it. This was one strange game of leap frog. I reached the town of Perth with the black car still a few lengths back. I decided to carry on to the restaurant where Maddie Ringer had agreed to meet me. I'd check to see if the car followed.

I pulled into a parking spot in front of Peter's Family Fare Restaurant on Gore Street. It was a grey limestone building with three large, square windows looking out on the street. I looked back down the street as I stepped onto the sidewalk, but didn't see the black car. I breathed easier. Maybe I imagined the driver's interest in me.

A woman in a yellow jogging suit lifted her head when I entered. I crossed the floor and slid into the booth across from her. "Thanks for meeting me today, Maddie," I said. "You were right about your yellow outfit being impossible to miss." She hadn't mentioned her flaming red hair, oversized green glasses, and dangling pink pig earrings. Any of those would have been equally as easy to spot.

Her smile was wide and friendly. "I'm sorry you had to come all this way. At least order breakfast. The food here is great."

"Don't mind if I do."

We ordered bacon, fried eggs, toast, and coffee. While we waited for the food to arrive, Maddie filled me in on her cousin, Laura Flint.

"Yeah, we grew up down the street from each other in Calgary. I'm three years older than her and also adopted. Our adoptive mothers are sisters."

"Were there other kids?"

"No. Just me and Laura. Needless to say, we were thrown together a lot growing up. At first I didn't mind. But once I hit the teen years, she was a pain." Maddie laughed. "She was such a needy kid, with no clue how to keep friends."

"How so?"

"Hanging on to me and everyone else like a leech. It got to be too much when I turned fifteen. I'm not proud to say that I began avoiding her. She used to call me all the time. She'd wait for me after school and I'd sneak out another door. Cruel really, looking back. I think that's why she ended up dating boys that year."

"She was what, twelve?"

"Yeah. Crazy, eh? She was called Loose Laura by the time she was thirteen. There was one guy—I can't remember his name now—that she seemed to settle on during high school. He dumped her in Grade Twelve, though. Splat! Like a hot potato. Surprised me, because they'd been all over each other all the time. The next thing I knew, she married this older guy Roger Flint."

"The one killed in the hunting accident."

"Yeah. That was a sad time. I went home for the funeral and Laura was all broken up. He left her a good amount of money and she started travelling. I was glad when she moved to Ottawa last year. We've gotten together a few times—my parents both died a few years back. It's nice to have some family around."

"She must have changed as an adult."

Maddie thought for a few seconds, then said, "She was different in many ways. Tougher, for sure, but still needy. She talked about what she owned and dropped names of people she knew. I think she still felt she had to prove something to me. In some ways, she was still that little girl who didn't belong."

Our food arrived and we stopped talking to eat. She'd been right when she said the food was good.

I pushed my plate away with a contented sigh and drank the last of my coffee. "You inherit her house and bank account?" I asked. I raised my head to watch Maddie's reaction.

She frowned. Her eyes lost their shine. "Maybe. I thought I would, but Laura didn't have a will. I have to wait to see if others come forward."

"How much money are we talking?" I couldn't remember seeing any bank statements in the paperwork that Rosie Brown had given me.

"I'm not sure. We haven't been kept informed and it seemed wrong to keep asking."

And maybe greedy.

"Two bills?" the waitress asked.

"One, and I'm paying," I said.

Maddie smiled. "Thanks. The other PI was too cheap to come to Perth. He gave me a two-minute phone call."

"And what did you tell him?"

"Not much. When he found out that I'd only seen Laura a couple of times in the last ten years, he lost interest."

"Laura's phone records show that you called her three times the week that she died. What did you talk about?"

Maddie's eyes widened as if I'd hit her in the stomach. She recovered by knocking over her coffee cup and jumping up from the table. "Now look what I've gone and done," she said. She grabbed napkins from the dispenser on the table and made a big show of cleaning up the small mess. Even the waitress came over to help tidy.

Maddie looked across at me when she finally sat back down. The smile this time had lost its warmth. "Where were we? Oh yes. The phone calls. I was trying to arrange a visit to stay with Laura in Ottawa. My only regret is that we never got together before she died. My last memory of her is from just before Christmas, when we exchanged gifts."

I was curious. "What did she give you?"

Maddie waved a hand in front of her face. "Oh, nothing big. Just a book on killing unwanted pests in the garden. There was a coupon that came with it."

I blinked.

Maddie's eyes filled with tears. "Laura knew how much I love flowers," she said. "The book was her way of being helpful. The really sad thing is that not even a year later, I was putting my roses on her grave."

A long, slow shiver travelled up my back. I tried to catch Maddie's eyes but she was getting up from the table with her face turned the other way. She'd scooted over to the counter before I had time to say anything in response.

I paid the bill and we walked out of the restaurant, Maddie keeping well ahead of me. She muttered something about being late and said a quick goodbye when we stepped outside. I could tell she had no intention of answering any more of my questions.

As a result I was more than a little surprised when Maddie called from across the street as I was unlocking my car. She was waving both arms above her head.

"Alex! Alex Dowd! That was the name of the guy she dated in high school." Maddie beamed and gave the thumbs up as if she'd just won the lottery.

"Great. Thanks for everything, Maddie." I returned her thumbs up. I unlocked my car and got in. I had a better idea now of who Laura Flint had been. She used men to feel loved. Paul Taylor was one in a string, and she had a hard time letting go. The police believed she'd gotten naked and snuck into his bed. He'd lost it and killed her. From everything Maddie had told me, Laura *could* have acted in that way. Paul Taylor might have had enough and killed her in a rage. I started the car.

However, another scenario was also taking shape in my mind. Maddie and her husband were only an hour's drive from Ottawa. They were keen to get their hands on Laura's money, but Laura looked at them as pests. The book was more than a gift, it was a message. And they'd taken a lesson from it and gotten rid of Laura before she got rid of them.

CHAPTER EIGHT

I checked my rear view mirror several times on my way back to Ottawa. The black car was nowhere in sight. I made good time and reached the Bentley sector in the west end right after lunch. The Taylor office building was tucked next to a sheet metal shop. From what I'd read, Taylor's company got off the ground making helicopters. They'd recently started making small planes as well. Paul Taylor's designs had made him very, very rich. The ground floor of the main building was a showroom. The offices were on the second.

A girl with a half-shaved head wearing shorts and work boots led me into a meeting room. Paul's backstabbing VPs Gordon Tate and Kyle Short were already inside waiting. They were bent over a file folder when I entered. Both stood and shook my hand before we all got comfortable around the table. Gordon had thinning blond hair and a round pleasant face; Kyle was tall and lean with shoulder length black hair and a full beard. Both wore jeans and dress shirts with their sleeves rolled up. They were in their early thirties, and eligible bachelors judging by their ringless left hands.

"Thanks for seeing me," I said.

Gordon and Kyle exchanged looks as if to see who should do the talking. Gordon must have lost the eye toss because he spoke first. Or maybe Kyle was just the follower that Paul Taylor had said he was.

"No problem, but we're not sure that we can tell you anything the police don't already know."

"That's okay. But I have to do my own investigation. I'm sorry to make you repeat everything." I opened my notebook and got out a pen. "I understand you're trying to buy out Paul Taylor's share of the company." No point dragging this out.

Gordon folded his arms across his chest. He glared at me. "We can't have a guy in prison for life running our business. We've already had clients cancel orders."

"But Paul hasn't been found guilty of anything yet."

Kyle spoke up. "He will be. There's nobody else who could have killed her."

I met his eyes. They were not pleased. "Neither of you seem to have liked him very much," I commented. "He told me that you were friends for a long time, Gordon."

Gordon's face tightened in anger. "We might have been friends, once. Paul Taylor didn't get where he was by being a nice guy. He stole my ideas and said they were his. He stepped on people when they got in his way. Killing a girlfriend so his wife wouldn't find out was just the next step up."

Shove in the knife and then turn the handle. "So where were the two of you the morning Laura Flint was murdered?" I asked.

They looked at each other again. Then Gordon turned to me and said, "We were both here working that morning, while Paul was out playing. We had a client in town from Boston. Paul took him golfing and we got to stay back and finish up his contract."

"Did anyone see the two of you that morning?"

"No. We were here alone, working through yet another Saturday while Taylor was off having fun." Gordon's face paled. "Not that killing Laura would have been fun. I meant the golf."

"Of course. How is business, by the way?"

Kyle smiled for the first time. "Good. Business is very good. We just had an outside firm do an audit and all is in order. This is turning into our best year yet." The two of them smiled at each other like a couple of cats sharing a bowl of cream.

And the only one standing in your way is on trial for murder. Gordon had motive and Kyle looked like he'd be eager to assist. And their alibis were each other. Not exactly rock solid. How far would they go to get rid of their boss? The glimmer of hope I felt for Paul Taylor after meeting with cousin Maddie was growing brighter.

"Well, those are all my questions for now." I stood. "I'll do a bit of digging before I come back to see you again. I guess the two of you won't be leaving town." I laughed but let the threat hang in the air.

I could tell by their eyes that neither of them found me all that funny.

· · · · · · · · · ·

I joined the heavy traffic heading home after the work day. I wasn't on my way home, though. I was heading back to the office to put in a few more hours of work.

I climbed the stairs and tried the office door. It was locked. Jada was probably home sleeping. She'd soon be getting ready for another night chasing after Dick the husband. I got out my key and let myself in.

The first thing I did was turn on the desk lamp and start the computer. While it booted up, I got myself a beer from the fridge. Then, I checked the two voice messages on the phone. Both were from people answering the office manager ad. Jada sure hadn't wasted any time. I'd been hoping that they were new clients asking for our services. Only three cases between us in a month and a half. If I didn't get Paul Taylor off, word would travel quickly. We'd be lucky to get any new business at all.

I typed a brief report for Rosie Brown and sent it to her by email. Then I turned my attention to my own files. These ones were for my own personal use and would never be shared with the client. It was where I wrote down all of my thoughts, feelings, and hunches. One small detail could later become the most important piece of the puzzle.

An hour into my work, I lifted my head. A banging noise had broken through my concentration. It sounded like it was coming from the stairwell. A prickle of alarm made me leap to my feet and cross to the door. I lifted a hand to turn the knob, but stopped to listen. The noise was louder and echoed up the empty stairwell.

I slowly turned the handle and looked out at the dimly lit landing. It took a moment for my eyes to adjust. Relief made me laugh out loud. It was only the door at the bottom of the stairs, swinging back and forth in the breeze. As I watched, it banged open against the brick wall outside.

"I thought I shut that," I said out loud. I sighed and climbed down the stairs. My knees still ached from my fall into the street. I pulled the door tight, making sure I heard the click of the latch. Somebody going by must have opened it and kept going. I had to stop being so jumpy.

After another hour hunched over the keyboard, I stood up and stretched.

Darkness filled the corners of the room. Night had crept in while I was working. I walked over to the window and looked out. The street lights were on. The white glow from store fronts and restaurants lit up the sidewalks. It was time to go home and make Dad some supper.

Gino was standing in the doorway of Roma's Pizza Shop when I stepped outside. He called my name and I walked over to stand in front of him.

"You're working late," he said. He was a short, round man with a grey crew cut and dancing black eyes.

"I'm on my way home now. It's been a long day."

"Say, my son Nick will be by tomorrow. Why don't you come meet him? He's a nice boy."

"And maybe I'm not such a nice girl."

Gino laughed. "You're a nice, nice girl, Anna Sweet. You and my Nickie are made for each other."

It was my turn to laugh. "How old is your son Nickie?"

"He's twenty-eight, but wise for his age."

"I'll think about it, Gino."

"Around noon tomorrow. Pizza on the house!"

"Good night, Gino." I raised a hand and kept walking toward my car.

A younger man *and* free food. Harder hearts had been won by less.

CHAPTER NINE

I almost kept driving when I saw Jimmy's car parked in Dad's driveway. "What are *you* doing here?" I muttered under my breath. I sighed and found a parking spot across the street. I stomped up the sidewalk and in the front door.

I found Dad and Jimmy sitting at the kitchen table eating Chinese food. Take-out boxes were spread across the table. Their plates were heaped with food that made me weak at the knees. Jimmy looked up at me and grinned.

"Grab a plate," he said.

"Don't mind if I do."

I took a plate out of the cupboard and sat down next to Dad. Jimmy slid the cartons across the table and I began scooping fried rice onto my plate. He was dressed in his navy police uniform and he'd slicked back his black curls with hair gel. He looked good.

I'd avoided being alone with Jimmy since my return to Ottawa a few months before. There was still something between us. It was in his eyes every time he looked at me. I knew he loved my sister Cheri, but we'd loved each other once. Why had he come here alone? He looked across at me and seemed to read my mind.

"I came to keep your dad company. Cheri took Evan to the pet store to buy a hamster. We promised him one for his birthday."

"Yeah, that's coming up, isn't it?" I moved on to the box of spareribs.

"Detective Shaw came by my office today," Jimmy added. "He tells me that you're trying to prove Paul Taylor innocent."

I stopped spooning ribs onto my plate and looked at him. "Now why would Shaw do that? Is he trying to warn me off?"

"No, I think he's actually concerned about you. He said that you're going to lose the Taylor case, because he's guilty. He also said that Jada Price was a trouble maker when she was a cop. You might not want to be connected with her. He wanted me to convince you to re-apply for a job with the force."

"Great to know that the two of you have my best interests at heart."

"I don't know if you've thought this through."

Dad held up a hand. "Don't you want to hear what I found out today, Anna?"

I continued dishing food onto my plate with jerky motions. "Yeah, Dad. What did you find out?" I glared at Jimmy and then loaded soy sauce onto my rice.

"After Laura Flint's husband died in the hunting accident, she went travelling. Paris, Rome, London . . . people lost track of her the last few years."

"Sounds like she was enjoying the single life." I licked my fingers. "Did she get a new boyfriend?"

"I couldn't pin anybody down on that."

"Well, I have a few more names for you to check out, Dad, if you're interested."

Dad pulled his notebook and pen from under a carton of chicken balls. "Go ahead."

"The two vice presidents of Taylor's company, Kyle Short and Gordon Tate. They're a bit too eager to see their boss rot in prison. Gordon Tate also seems to think Taylor took credit for his designs. I'd also like you to look into the bank account of Laura's cousin Maddie and her husband. I have a feeling it's on the low side."

"Anybody else?"

I thought for a second. It was nice to see Dad's mind busy with something besides being sick. One more name popped into my head. "Alex Dowd. He was Laura's high school boyfriend. See if you can find out what he's been doing all these years." That should keep Dad busy.

"Okay," Dad said. He pushed away his full plate and stood. "I'll get started on these."

"Wait! I didn't mean to start working on them now. You need to eat."

"That's okay. I'm not hungry. I can heat the food up later."

I frowned and watched him leave. Had he lost his appetite again? Was he feeling sick and not telling me?

Jimmy looked up from his plate. "He ate two spring rolls and a bowl of hot and sour soup before you got here."

I met his eyes. They were warm hazel and flecked with green. "I just worry about him," I said.

"I know."

"I don't know what I'll do if he doesn't make it through this."

"He will and so will you." Jimmy paused for a moment. "I didn't mean to upset you about Shaw. I don't want to see you get hurt." He tucked his head back over his plate. "It's just that I've never stopped worrying about you, either."

CHAPTER TEN

D ad was still sleeping when I left the house the next morning at nine a.m. I'd heard him up half the night talking on the phone and clicking keys on his laptop. I left him a note to call me later.

I drove toward Hintonburg to check in at the office. I was hoping to catch up with Jada before I headed back to Rockcliffe. First, I made a stop at Fil's Diner for breakfast. Fil's had that sixties feel— booths and a long counter with stools in front of the open grill. The place was busy as usual, but I found a seat at the counter. I ordered French toast, sausages, and coffee, and read the Ottawa paper while I waited.

The front page had a photo of Katie Taylor leaving the jail. Her eyes were hidden behind dark sunglasses. Her lips were painted bright red. The article talked about the murder and the upcoming trial, but it focused on the Taylors' marriage. It was the first time Katie had agreed to be interviewed.

She'd even given the paper private family photos. She'd told the reporter that Paul was fifteen years older than her. They met on a beach in Mexico and married three months later. She believed in love at first sight. She loved Paul even more today than she had when he asked her to be his wife.

I tossed the paper onto the counter. Katie's interview left a sick, sugary taste in my mouth. All that gooey love when Paul Taylor had just slept with their neighbour. Was this woman for real?

My food arrived. The waitress saw Katie's picture and said, "Hard to believe her husband fooled around on her. Most men would do anything to have her as their wife. She sure does love the bum."

"She certainly appears to."

I ate slowly and had a second cup of coffee. All the while, I was trying to understand how a woman with Katie Taylor's looks and career could settle for a cheating husband. Her words of undying love were even stranger when I considered she'd all but moved out the month before. Call me jaded, but I was having trouble swallowing her new-found devotion.

I paid my bill and stepped outside. The morning was cool but sunny, the sky deep blue. I inhaled deeply and tried to focus on the day ahead. The more I looked into this case, the more questions popped up like dandelions. I was going to have to get busy tracking down answers before the entire investigation got away from me.

··········

Jada was on the phone when I climbed the stairs to our office. I took a seat on the other side of the desk and waited for her to finish the call. Less than a minute later, she hung up and grinned at me. "Free at last! I've convinced the wife that Dick is faithful. No more nights chasing him from bar to bar."

"How did you find out that he's not cheating?"

"Easy. I sat on the stool next to him and asked. It's amazing what strangers will tell you after a few drinks in a bar. He said that he's been filling in time by hanging out with the guys. He was celebrating last night because he starts a new job as a security guard on the weekend. It means he can work nights and be with his wife during the day. He's going to tell her when she gets off shift. He was thrilled that he's going to get to spend more time with her."

"Well, that's sweet."

"Isn't it? She feels bad for doubting him." Jada leaned back and relaxed in her chair. "So, what's up with your case?"

"A few leads. I'm still working on Laura Flint's history. I'll start looking at Katie Taylor this afternoon. I can't say that I've got anything concrete."

"Let me know if you need help. Today, I'm writing my report for Dick's wife. Then I have four people coming in to interview for the office manager job. After all that, home for some sleep."

"I should be fine. Dad's helping me with research."

"That's great that he's feeling up to it." Jada knew all about Dad's cancer scare. I suspected that she also knew he was the reason I was sticking around Ottawa.

I started toward the door. I stopped with my hand on the door knob. "If you get hungry, drop down to Gino's around noon. Tell him that I sent you. I hear he's handing out free pizza."

....

Peggy Plum opened Laura Flint's front door and invited me in. The first thing I noticed was Peggy's rust red hair, shoulder length and permed into a tumble of tight curls. An orange dress hugged her two hundred pounds of curves. Plum Pickings Real Estate had been selling homes in Rockcliffe since before I was born. Peggy was the owner and poster girl.

"Heck of a shame about Laura Flint," she said. "I sold her this house just six months ago."

Peggy led me down the hall into the living room. Two chairs and a lamp stood in front of the bay window. The rest of the large space was empty.

"Is most of her furniture in storage?" I asked.

"No. This is about it. There's a bed and dresser upstairs in one of the bedrooms, a table and chairs in the kitchen, a closetful of clothes and some costume jewelry. Nothing worth very much."

"Laura lived here for half a year. I would have thought she'd have more . . . stuff."

"I guess some people like to travel light."

"That's one way of looking at it."

Peggy led me into the big, sunny kitchen at the back of the house. It opened into a dining area. Three steps down was the family room. Both rooms were empty.

"She could have held barn dances in here," I said, walking across the family room to the sliding glass doors. They opened into the backyard. An in-ground pool took up the left side of the yard. It was filled with brown water and leaves. The three garden beds were mainly growing weeds and the grass between them was knee high. I couldn't see any way that the yard would have become this overgrown in six weeks. "I would have thought Laura would hire a gardener or pool boy to look after the yard," I said.

Peggy crossed the room to stand next to me. "Between you and me, I don't think she had much money. She had enough for the down payment, but my friend at the bank tells me her account was nearly empty."

Peggy would have her spies everywhere, of course. She'd kept her business booming while others went under. "Who lived here before Laura?"

"An older man. He fell last winter and broke his hip and had to go into a home. He was losing it, though. Kept saying someone pushed him. Anyway, Laura came with an offer the day his house went on the market."

I stood very still. Maybe the old gentleman hadn't been losing it. Maybe he really had been pushed. What were the odds of Laura Flint showing up the day after he broke his hip? It was the second accident to work out in her favour. In the first, her husband had died from a stray bullet while out hunting. She'd ended up with all his money and her freedom.

Was Laura in fact the evil one? Maybe that was something I'd have to consider. But she hadn't been in the woods when her husband was shot. And she sure hadn't smothered herself in the Taylors' bed. Was somebody else involved? If it wasn't Paul Taylor, who else could it be?

We finished a tour of the upstairs. Only one of the five bedrooms had furniture. I didn't find anything of interest in her few possessions, but hadn't planned to. I knew the police had already been through the place.

"Thanks for everything, Peggy," I said when we reached the front door. "If I'm ever looking to buy a house in Rockcliffe, you'll be the first one I call."

She smiled. We both knew that would never happen. "Well, I might have a bigger house next door on the market soon, the way things are going."

We both looked over the cedar hedge to the Taylors' house. The look on Peggy's face reminded me of a vulture circling a dying animal.

I waited until she shut the door before scooting across the lawn to Katie Taylor's front door. I rang the bell and waited. I thought I heard music coming from inside. When a minute went by and nobody came, I rang the bell again. It chimed deep in the house. Still, nobody came to open the door. Either Katie was busy or she didn't feel like seeing anybody. That wouldn't stop me from poking into her past, though. I was already late for my next meeting downtown.

CHAPTER ELEVEN

A skinny boy with large black-framed glasses and dressed in a pink shirt pointed me to the white leather couch. "It shouldn't be long," he said.

I made myself comfortable and flipped through fashion magazines. A steady line of tall, underfed girls trooped in and out of Maggie Wren's office while I waited my turn. The room smelled of coffee and sweet vanilla. At first, I found the smells pleasant. After half an hour, I had a head ache.

At last, the guy on the desk put down the phone and called over. "Anna Sweet, Ms. Wren will see you now."

I'd been reading an article on how to improve myself in five easy steps. The first three were on how to lose weight. The fourth step involved learning how to say no. I guess that was learning how to say no to food, if the first three steps meant anything. I'd keep the fifth step as a surprise. One should always leave room for improvement. I jumped up and headed for the closed door. I pushed it open and took a look around.

A glass-topped desk sat in the middle of the inner office under three long, narrow skylights. The furniture was sleek and modern; low red and grey chairs were artfully placed on a white shag carpet. The wall facing me was red brick with a row of square windows near the ceiling. Framed photos of models lined the other walls, which had been painted a charcoal colour.

Maggie Wren fit into the decor. She was another tall woman, elegant in a black dress and boots. Her silver hair was cut into a short bob, her red lips a pop of colour. Her arms jangled with gold bracelets as she lifted a hand to shake mine. I cringed as I remembered what I'd put on that morning. I'd found the only clean pair of jeans rolled into a ball in my closet, then chosen a long blue turtleneck to cover the rip in the back pocket. I'd topped these off with my black leather jacket, mainly to hide the ketchup stain on the turtleneck. There was no doubt. I was going to have to take myself shopping when this case was over.

Maggie led me to a low red couch under the bank of windows. I lowered myself with care. I was surprised to find the seat comfortable.

"We were shocked to hear that Katie Taylor's husband was charged with murder," Maggie began. "Such an awful tragedy. We all adore Katie."

"I understand she began working for you early last year."

"That's correct. February to be exact. As you might know, most of her career was with a large agency in New York City. She joined us when she married Paul and moved to Ottawa. That was about five years ago. She stopped taking jobs three years ago, but decided to come back recently. It only lasted a few months, though. In July, she said no more travel. I have no idea why."

"Do you know the reason she came back in February? After being away so long from the business?"

"Katie told me that she was bored at home. She stopped work the first time to have a family. She told me that she got cold feet because Paul was always working. She didn't want to raise their children alone. I don't think they were getting along last year, to be honest."

"I'm told that they were happier the last few months. She'd agreed to try for a baby again in July. That must be why she didn't want to travel."

"If you say so." Maggie didn't look convinced.

"Katie was away on location for most of May and June. Can you tell me where?"

Maggie shook her head. "You have it wrong. Katie did a two-day shoot in Toronto in May and a week in Montreal. That was it. Most of our big jobs are for younger models. Katie worked out in the gym daily and was in great shape, but still, she *was* thirty years old."

"Are you sure that's all her jobs those months? Could she have been working for another agency?" I thought back to my notes. Paul Taylor had told me that Katie was away for most of those two months. That was why he'd started up with Laura.

"No, her contract says that I have to approve work from other agencies. One moment." Maggie walked over to her computer and clicked open a file. She printed it off and handed me the copy. I scanned the dates and locations. Sure enough, Katie had been on two shoots for a total of seven days. The question was, who was lying, Katie or Paul?

Paul might have padded his wife's time away to make me believe he had reason for an affair. Katie left him alone so often, he got lonely. Katie's actions led to him sleeping with the neighbour. *A cheater's logic.* On the other hand, Katie might have lied to Paul because ... why? Why did most women lie to their husbands? Yet, she'd cut back on shoots a second time to start a family. She was standing by him and insisting he was innocent.

I was getting more than a little confused.

I thanked Maggie Wren and headed for the door. If I hurried, I'd just have time to make it to the toy store before it closed. Even tracking down a killer needed to take a back seat to finding a birthday gift for my one and only nephew.

··········

I'd just finished parking my car on the main street of Westboro, the neighbourhood that butted onto Hintonburg, when Dad called on my cellphone. I leaned against the car while we talked.

"Anna," he barked. "I'm ready to file my report."

I smiled. Sometimes, I found him awfully cute. "All set, Dad. Let me know what you've got."

"Well, the two VPs, Gordon Tate and Kyle Short, are a couple of boring fellows. I couldn't dig up dirt on either one. Both grew up in Ottawa and signed on with Taylor five years ago. Neither is married. Work appears to be all they live for."

"Not what I was hoping for."

"Their bank accounts are solid. No strange activity."

"Anything else?"

"No, but I'll keep looking. I also located the high school boyfriend. Alex Dowd. Last known address is New York City."

"Really? How long has he lived there?"

"No idea. I have an address and another army buddy on his way down to check it out."

"Where does this army buddy live?"

"Montreal."

"Dad, maybe that's asking too much." Especially since this was just work to keep Dad busy.

"Nonsense. He's happy to do it. Said he couldn't imagine anything more fun. He's going to report in tonight."

I'd created a monster. "Well, ask him to submit his bill for gas and expenses. I want to pay him."

"No need, but I'll let him know. Where are you now?"

I looked across the street at the toy store. "I'm about to find a birthday gift for Evan."

"Great. The party's tomorrow night. Cheri's bringing the food."

"I hope she's having someone else make it."

"You and me both."

CHAPTER TWELVE

The next day was one of those unexpected hot, humid ones that Ottawa is famous for. Dad warned me to put on light clothes as he passed by my bedroom door. "Going to be a scorcher," he called. "The weather is getting crazy. Global warming."

I found a white T-shirt and tan summer slacks. I pulled my leather sandals from the back of the closet. I would have rather worn shorts but it was a work day.

I joined Dad in the kitchen. He'd already made the coffee and was scrambling eggs at the stove. "My turn to feed you," he said.

I got a cup of coffee and cut some bread for toast. Dad shooed me over to the table while he finished making breakfast. He'd started cooking after Mom died, when I was eleven. He'd stay up half the night trying to make her recipes, until he mastered them.

"So what's our plan of attack today?" Dad asked as he slid a plate in front of me. He'd added a side of berries and melon to go with the eggs. He poured himself a coffee and joined me with his own plate.

"I'm debating who to visit first, Paul or Katie Taylor. Their stories are off a bit and I want to find out why. What about you, Dad?"

"I'm going to keep digging on those two vice presidents. From what you told me, Gordon Tate thinks Paul Taylor screwed him over. That kind of bad feeling grows over time. It can turn to hate real quick. And my army buddy should be in New York City by now. He'll be reporting in later today."

"Sounds good. I'm going to find out more about Katie Taylor's activities over the past year. I'm heading over to speak with her now. I called last night and she said she'd give me a few minutes. I'll also try to get the name of a friend or two of hers, to find out if she told them anything about her marriage."

Dad's notebook and pen appeared out of nowhere. "Just making a note to track down Maddie Ringer's bank. We sure have lots of lines of enquiry going on. It's easy to forget one." When he finished writing, he looked at me with his sharp blue eyes. "What will you do if after all this you find Paul Taylor really did murder Laura Flint?"

I knew by the way he asked that he thought Taylor could be the killer. "First, I'll send his lawyers my report," I said with a smile. "And then, I'll start looking for a waitress job."

"Jimmy says they'd hire you back on the force if you're interested."

"I know. If you recall, he told me that the other night when he was over. I'll think about it, Dad." I picked up my empty plate. Why was it that just thinking about returning to the force felt like a failure? I made my voice lighter than I felt. "Let's hope we catch us a killer today, Dad. And let's really hope that killer is not my client."

....

Katie Taylor let me into the front hallway but didn't invite me any further into her house. "I have a busy day," she said. "I have to stand in for Paul at a meeting with Gordon, Kyle, and a client after I visit Paul in jail." She was wearing a sleeveless green dress and black sandals. She smelled like expensive French perfume. "Have you found out anything to help my husband?"

"I'm following up on several leads." True without committing myself. "Did you ever meet Laura Flint's cousin, Maddie Ringer?"

"No. Laura told me when she moved next door that she had a cousin in Perth who was after her money. She didn't appear worried about it. She seemed to think the whole thing was a joke."

"So, she wasn't worried about Maddie trying to hurt her?"

"God, no. Laura called her a lazy lump." Katie laughed. Her white teeth were straight and perfect. The woman's beauty had no flaws that I could see. She tossed back her cascade of midnight black hair and looked at the diamond-studded watch on her arm.

"I'm curious about your recent modelling jobs," I said.

Her green eyes lifted to mine. "Oh? I can't see how that helps Paul."

"I'm trying to cover every detail of your lives together. It helps me to narrow down my search."

She smiled. "Of course. What did you want to know exactly?"

"After speaking with Maggie Wren . . ."

"You spoke with my modelling agency?" Her voice rose and her green eyes opened wider. "Do you even know how to investigate? Paul is on trial for murder and you're wasting time looking at my career?"

"I know this might not seem important, but . . ." I let my voice trail away. "Paul told me that you were on shoots for the months of May and June. Maggie said you only had seven days of work during those two months. I wondered where you were."

"I don't see that that is any of your business." She crossed her arms in front of her chest. One foot tapped up and down on the floor. "If you must know, Paul and I were having problems in our marriage. I took some time away to think. I was deciding whether or not to leave him."

"You returned and said you were ready to start a family."

"That's correct. I realized that I love him."

"You still haven't told me where you were for May and June."

"No, I haven't. Now, if you'll excuse me, I'm late for my workout." She bent down to pick up her gym bag. "When I visit Paul later today, I'm going to suggest that he find another PI. One who isn't wasting money on finding out information that has nothing to do with his case."

. . . .

That went well. I hadn't even had a chance to ask her about her friends. Watching Katie Taylor pull out of her driveway, I could only wonder what had gotten her so upset.

I probably had one more day to figure out the Taylor case before I was fired. The worst part was that maybe Katie was right. Maybe I didn't know what I was doing. Dad and I were chasing leads that led nowhere.

I drove toward the jail where Paul was being held. He was counting on me to come up with something. I thought about quitting the case before Katie made him fire me. I turned onto the Parkway and glanced in the rear view mirror. A black car with tinted windows pulled in right behind me. The front licence plate was missing. It looked like the same car that had followed me to Perth. I sped up and the driver stayed right behind me, much too close for comfort. If I braked suddenly, they would have hit my bumper. My heart beat double time as fear pulsed through me. I pushed harder on the gas pedal and my car leapt forward.

When I checked my rear view again, the black car was still right behind me. I felt a sudden jolt as it rammed my back bumper. "Back off!" I screamed just as it struck me again. I struggled not to wrench the steering wheel off course. I checked the rear view. The car was pulling into the next lane over. Before I could react, the car had pulled alongside me. I sped up more, but it kept pace, edging my car closer to the shoulder of the highway. Our side mirrors collided and mine snapped off like a broken wing.

The exit ramp was just up ahead. I pressed my foot as hard as I could on the gas pedal and got a slight jump on the black car. I was almost even with the ramp when I let off the gas and pumped the brake. The black car shot ahead as I swerved onto the ramp. I just managed to keep my car from spinning into the concrete barricade. I screeched to a stop at the stop sign at the end of the ramp. I struggled to control my breathing and my shaking hands. I checked behind me. The ramp was empty for the moment.

I turned left onto the main highway and drove as fast as I dared. When I exited onto Innes Road, the black car was still nowhere in sight. I pulled over and waited to make sure the car was really gone. It took a full minute for my heart to feel like it wasn't beating its way out of my chest.

That's when my cellphone rang.

CHAPTER THIRTEEN

"Is this a good time to file my report?" Dad asked.

I watched cars speeding by. "Sure. Why not?"

"My army buddy called. He's done some snooping. Alex Dowd was living in an apartment in New York City last year. He spent a lot of time working out in the local gym but didn't have a paying job. He moved to Ottawa six months ago."

I sat up straighter. "Six months ago, Laura Flint moved next door to the Taylors."

"I seemed to recall that. My buddy sent a recent photo of Alex. Another guy in the building took it at a party. I'm about to send it to you."

"Okay. I'll have a look when our call is over. Anything else?"

"Dowd didn't have a job but he wore expensive clothes. He worked out and got invited to parties with famous people. A woman used to visit him but she didn't live with him. She's in the photo, too."

"Interesting."

"Gotta go," Dad said. "I've got a cake in the oven. Don't forget Evan's party."

"Right. What time?"

"They'll be arriving at four. Dinner's at six."

"I'll be there."

I clicked on Dad's message and opened up the photo. Alex Dowd was in his early thirties, blond, buff, and tanned. He was holding a beer in one hand, a big grin on his face. I leaned in for a closer look. The hair colour was lighter but there was no doubt in my mind: the woman that Alex had his other arm draped around was none other than his high school sweetheart Laura Flint. She was clinking her beer bottle against his and her head was tucked into the hollow of his neck. She looked happy, relaxed, and very much in love.

Of course. Laura Flint's high school sweetheart. Who better to help her kill her husband and break an old man's hip? I looked down the road and thought about the black car that had tried to ram me off the road. I remembered how the push had felt that landed me in the middle of the busy street. It must have been him. And if so, Alex Dowd was one nasty piece of work. I had no doubt he would have killed Laura in a heartbeat, once her money ran out.

I lowered my phone. Pieces of the puzzle were finally sliding into place. It was time to set the final trap.

· · · · · · · · · ·

Paul Taylor looked even more tired and dejected than on my first visit. He hadn't combed his silver hair recently. His shoulders were more rounded. The sight of me didn't appear to help his mood. "So?" His voice was empty of energy.

"I believe you were set up. I can't prove it yet, though. I'll need your help."

Paul lifted his head and studied my face. Something flickered in his eyes. Something hard. "Who?" he asked.

"I'm not sure yet. I want to throw out some bait. You have to be prepared not to like who we reel in."

He thought over what I'd said before nodding. "Someone else deserves to be in a cell; not me. I have no problem putting away one of my friends. What do you need?"

"Katie is coming to see you today before she meets with Kyle and Gordon. She's going to ask you to take me off the case. Tell her that I've got a lead that you want to see through. Let it drop that the lead has to do with Laura Flint's boyfriend Alex Dowd from high school. Also, tell your wife that I'm working late tonight at my office. If you can, slip in that my partner is away."

"That's it?"

"Yeah. That ought to do it."

Paul Taylor was no fool. "Are you saying that you think my wife had something to do with this? Because that would be insane. She's been the only one to stand by me. We're planning a family together."

"No, I'm not saying that at all. She's bound to share your update with the vice presidents. This way, she doesn't really know anything and she's protected."

Paul was distracted enough to buy my explanation. "Fine," he said.

I called for the guard and made my escape. I didn't want to give Paul Taylor time to dig any deeper into my request.

....

I bought some lunch from a Westboro food truck and sat at their picnic table to eat. I made a few calls between munching on French fries and a burger. The sun was like a heat lamp on my face. Too bad this one day heat wave wouldn't last. My last call was to Dad. I told him not to hold supper for me. I'd do my best to get home when I could. Hopefully, there would still be some birthday cake left.

My next stop was a spy equipment store. I bought a video camera hidden in a digital clock. The sound and picture quality were amazing. The spy clock used a battery and would sit on the desk in our office, ready to record. I looked at the spy watches and other high-tech toys. I'd be back when I had more money.

It was nearly five o'clock when I climbed the stairs to the Storm Investigations office. The sun had started to sink lower in the sky and a chill had replaced the day's heat. I unlocked the door and left it unlocked. I hoped that Paul Taylor had given Katie my message. If I was right, the driver of the black car would soon be paying me a visit.

CHAPTER FOURTEEN

I kept busy typing my report for Paul's lawyers. It gave me time to review the facts and to think. All the while, I was listening for footsteps on the stairs. As time went by, it got harder to concentrate. The clock struck seven and I thought about calling the whole thing off. I looked toward the other room, now completely in darkness. The door was half open, revealing the empty space. If no one showed up, I was going to look mighty foolish.

I decided to give it a bit more time. Ten minutes later, my patience was rewarded. The stairs creaked as someone's weight shifted on the old wooden steps.

Show time.

The door to my office silently swung open and Alex Dowd stepped inside. He made a quick check of the room and shut the door firmly behind him. He was wearing leather gloves, a black jacket, and a ball cap.

I pretended to be surprised. "Can I help you?" I asked.

"I think you can."

He walked toward the desk and stood a few feet in front of it. He took off his baseball cap and smiled. The word that came to mind was hot. Alex Dowd was definitely a man that women would do bad things for. Messy blond hair, bleached almost white from the sun, square jaw, eyes that could melt butter, and a strong body. Animal heat steamed off of him like a boiling kettle.

"You've been talking about me to people," he said.

"I might have a few questions for you, Alex. Why don't you take a seat?" I pointed to the chair next to him. It was hard to get a read on what he planned to do. I had to keep him talking.

"I'll stand, thanks. Ask away."

"Why did you kill her?"

"You don't waste any time. I guess you're referring to Laura. How did you know we were still in touch?"

"I had a source in New York City. They tracked the two of you to an apartment building. Laura moved to Ottawa six months ago and so did you."

"That doesn't prove anything. We ran into each other a few years ago."

"Really? I think that if I do some more digging, I'll find that the two of you were together right after her husband was shot by a mystery hunter. You lived the good life on her husband's money."

"I'm not admitting to anything." He moved half a step closer. One hand was in his jacket pocket. I tried to keep my eyes on his face. "Let's say that *if* I killed Laura's husband, she would have come up with the plan. Laura was tired of being married to an old fart."

"I think you both planned it *before* she married him. The two of you carried on behind his back and waited for the right time to get rid of him."

He shrugged. "Show me your proof, lady."

"I intend to. So, your money...or I should say, Laura's dead husband's money, was running out. The two of you decided to con some other rich sucker out of their money. That's why you weren't living together in New York or here. It's hard to pick up somebody rich when you have a partner at home. God forbid, either of you got a job or scaled back your lifestyle. Who came up with the plan to target the Taylors?"

"*If* we had a plan, Laura was the one with the big ideas."

"It's easy to blame a dead woman. What, did she get jealous when you actually fell for Katie Taylor?

Did Laura tell you she'd let you go over her dead body?"

A puzzled look came into his eyes. He wrinkled his forehead as if trying to place her. "Katie Taylor?"

"Too late to pretend she's not involved. Your arrival here tonight confirms the two of you are in on this together."

His eyes got a little less happy. "The problem you leave me," he said, "is that you aren't going to let this go, are you?"

I shook my head. "Nope."

Dowd nodded. "So be it." He took another step closer, at the same time pulling a hunting knife out of his jacket pocket. The desk was still between us. I got to my feet and pushed back my chair.

Dowd stopped and held up both hands in a shrug. The knife glinted in the light from the desk lamp. "Believe me, nobody was more surprised than me that I fell hard for Katie Taylor. Laura would never have stood for it if I left her. She didn't like being on her own. Let's say that she could have made my life very difficult. As time went by, I came to realize that I needed both Laura and Paul out of the way so that I could have Katie *and* the money."

"Katie was in on it," I said. I wanted to hear it from him.

"Katie had to go back with Paul and convince him that she loved him. We couldn't chance him cutting her out of his bank account." He took another step toward the desk. The knife was starting to make me nervous. I'd also gotten enough on tape to nail them. "Shaw!" I yelled. I looked Dowd in the eyes. "I wouldn't do that if I were you. You're in enough trouble already."

Detective Shaw and Jada burst out of the little room where they'd been listening in the dark. Shaw had his handgun pointed at Dowd. "Put down the knife, Dowd. He looked over at me. "Nice work, Sweet."

"Anytime." I sank back into my chair. I looked at Jada. "If we keep this business going, we should really think about upping our life insurance policy."

CHAPTER FIFTEEN

Jada waited until Shaw and Dowd were out the door before she leapt across the floor. She grabbed me around the waist and lifted me into the air. "I can't believe you got Taylor off! This is going to make the national news. Storm Investigations will be drowning in work!"

I laughed as we jumped up and down. I hadn't felt so happy about anything in a long time. The new clock on our desk caught my eye.

"Look at the time! Evan will be waiting for his present." I grabbed my jacket from the back of my chair. "We'll have to celebrate later."

Jada walked with me to the door. "I was going to tell you about the person I hired today. In all the excitement, I almost forgot."

I paused. "Do I know her?"

"Not a her; a him. Nick Roma begins Monday. He said that he can't wait to meet you. Oh yeah, and his dad Gino says hi."

· · · · · · · · · ·

"Another piece?" Dad asked. He waved the knife in the air, waiting for me to say yes.

"Why not?" I said and held up my plate. Dad slid a chunk of chocolate cake onto it and a smaller one on his own. I scooped out the ice cream.

"Thanks for holding off on dessert," I said, licking the spoon. "You bake a great cake."

"Well, Evan wouldn't have it any other way. He sure liked the kite you gave him. It's a beauty."

"I can't wait to get him outside running around."

Dad and I were sitting at the kitchen table. Jimmy, Cheri, and Evan had just gone home so that Jimmy could get ready for the night shift.

"Dad, I want to thank you for all your help with this case. I wouldn't have put it all together if you hadn't kept digging."

"Gave me something to do." Dad's voice was gruff but I think he was secretly pleased. "I was mighty surprised that Katie Taylor was in on framing her husband. Good work figuring that out."

"Well, I found it impossible to believe she'd forgive him so easily for sleeping with Laura Flint."

"I can't think of too many women who would have let that slide past."

"Especially not an independent woman who looks like Katie Taylor." I checked my watch. "Shaw sent some cops over to pick her up. She should be putting on her new orange jump suit right about now."

Dad swallowed the last of his tea and stood up. "Well, tomorrow is chemo day so I'd better go get some sleep."

"What time do we have to be at the clinic?"

"Early. Six a.m. I'll be taking a cab."

"No, I'm driving you, Dad."

"There's no need."

"But I want to. I'll be up by five."

Dad looked down at me for a few seconds. A smile came and went. "I must have done something right in my life," he said finally. He nodded at me before turning and walking out of the kitchen. "Good night, Anna," he called over his shoulder. "Don't forget to lock up."

"Good night, Dad."

I love you too.